SO DO YOU LOVE ME OR NOT

Morgan Mosley

The characters and events portrayed in this book are fictitious. Any similarity to real persons, living or dead, is coincidental and not intended by the author.

ISBN- 9798842868179

Printed in the United States of America

Without you I would not have gotten this far! I thank each and everyone one of you reading this now. You took time from your day for me and I am forever greatful.

CONTENTS

Title Page
Copyright
Dedication
Rick 1
Jerome 8
Rick 14
Jerome 20
Rick 26
Jerome 32
Rick 38
Jerome 44
Rick 51
Jerome 57
Rick 64
Jerome 70
Rick 74
Jerome 80

Rick 85
Jerome 91
Rick 97
Jerome 103
Rick 109
Jerome 116
Shae~The End 123

RICK

Episode One

Not fully awake, I groaned faintly into my pillow. My head pounded like someone was hammering it with a nail. I tried fluttering my eyes open but only succeeded one at a time. I tossed on myself on my bed and blinked rapidly as I stared at my environment. It took me a full minute to finally remember where I was. It sucked, for I couldn't recognize my own room. I yanked my comforter from my body. The force was too great; I threw it completely off the bed. Another groan escaped from my throat as I grabbed my head in both hands and let out a shrill. Hangovers were the worst, and that was the reason why I hated them. To worsen my case, I couldn't recall the motive behind my drunken spree. I couldn't recall anything.

My eyes voluntarily spun to my bedpost, and I scrambled to get the aspirin and the glass of water on it. I downed it within a second and lolled on the bedrest, allowing the aspirin to take full effect.

Five minutes passed, and I bounced out of bed with rejuvenated energy. I drew out the curtain, and when the sun rays hit my face, my headache returned. I sighed, appreciating the fact that it was so much better than when I woke up. Putting on my cotton robe, I made my way out of the bedroom. The sweet aroma of bacon, sausage, and eggs filled my nostrils as I descended the stairs. My favorite women were both downstairs. Miranda was in her crib, playing with the toys fixed in the crib.

“Good morning,” I said, advancing toward Shae. She didn't turn around, and I greeted her again, louder this time. She finally spun, and a panic attack swirled in me. Her eyes were bloodshot, with bags underneath. Her face was red and puffy, like she'd been crying or didn’t sleep the entire night. But deep down, I knew it was the former. “Babe, are you okay?”

“Oh, you're up already.” She sniffed, then focused on her meal. She filled my plate with enough food. Here’s your breakfast. She said with a weak smile and wiped her nose with a tissue she picked from her robe.

“Shae, what's wrong with you?” I ignored the food in front of me to the demise of my howling tummy. I leaned closer and touched her face, but she stepped backward and averted her gaze.

“Yes, I'm fine. It's a cold. You know how those things are. Please have your breakfast.”

“Shae, I know you. This isn't a cold. What's wrong with you, baby?” It hurts to see her like this. It even hurt more being clueless about what made her like this.

“You really don't remember anything from last night?” She asked, blinking back the tears. She gripped the edge of the counter for support and looked intently at me. Her stare only broke when a single tear fell from her left eye.

“What happened? I've been trying to remember, but I can't.” I tapped my forehead gently in an attempt to recall anything, even if it were a single minor detail from last night.

“Oh, okay.” She whispered. “It's nothing, Rick. Just have your breakfast. Can you keep an eye on Miranda for me today? I have a few errands to run.”

“Shae.” I grabbed her hands, but her reflexes were faster. She dodged and climbed upstairs, leaving only the thudding sounds of her slippers.

When Shae left, I spent a full hour trying to dig up events from the previous night. Miranda clearly gave me a hard time, but I dealt with her amicably. With a last option swimming in my head, I picked up my phone and dialed my best friend's number.

“Dennis, are you busy?” I asked, letting out a groan as Miranda's tears flooded through my ears.

“No, you want me to come over?” He asked.

“No, what happened last night? I remember you were with me.”

“Yes, we went to the bar and had a few drinks. You had a lot to drink. I offered to take you home, but you said no. Even humiliated me in front of everybody there." I could sense the frown on his face.

I shut my ears as the memory slipped into my head. "Yeah, about that, I'm sorry, man."

"It's okay, I understand. You were bent up about your girlfriend, Shae. Saying you were scared she'd found out about what happened with Melanie."

I blew out a breath, raking my hands through my hair. Miranda continued to wail from the living room. I paced the room as reality dawned on me.

"Why, what happened, man?"

"I don't know, man. I think I might have said or done something. Shae has been crying since God knows when." I sighed.

"Oh shit, you don't think you said anything, did you? You think you confessed to her or something? Man, that sucks."

"I don't know. She won't say anything. She won't even speak to me. She made me breakfast and just left for some errands. I'm fucking worried, man."

"Man, I told you to tell her the truth a long time ago. But you didn't listen. Instead, you went ahead with that stupid plan."

"I love her, man. I fucking love her." I sank to the floor and felt tears streaming down my face. "I don't want to lose her."

"I understand, man. Right now, we can only hope you didn't expose yourself last night. What are you going to do now?"

"I don't know. I can try and get her talking just to know how much damage I caused." I bit my nails in frustration. Unable to contain Miranda's tears any longer, I stormed downstairs.

"Okay, Miranda, you need to be quiet. I'm really tired right now." She stopped crying when I popped my face in her crib. "Thank you."

"Or you could just tell her the truth. You can't hide this forever."

"Melanie has left Long Island. It shouldn't be a bother."

"Still, man, you need to tell Shae. Or you will lose her."

Dennis was right, but the truth was, I wasn't ready to tell her the truth yet.

I wasn't ready for the aftermath.

JEROME

<u>*Episode Two*</u>

The door slammed loudly, and I heard a creak in it. I stood still, wrapped in my towel, staring at the empty void around me. The light that previously glistened in the room dimmed drastically. It felt like I'd been pushed into a 50s monochrome movie. My gaze fell on my bed with my phone vibrating softly on it. Pacified, I grabbed it only to discover my wife's name on it. Mixed emotions swirled in me. Anger, frustration, agitation, and angst muddled against my flesh. I watched my phone's screen turn off and took a step, every vein in my body pulling me to run after Melanie.

Truth was, I didn't mean to utter those cruel, demeaning words to her. All my life, retaliation had been my strongest pursuit. Having suffered from bullying at a younger age, I defended myself in brutal ways. I made sure when you hit me, I hit you ten times stronger. And that was what happened with Melanie.

I knew I didn't love her, but I cared for her. The day I discovered she was seventeen was a blow to my heart. Initially, my intentions towards her were pure. I had the plan to help her because I wanted to. I understood how it felt when life crashed you underneath the earth's surface. I just wanted to help her. From the start, my intuition screamed at me. It was too obvious she ran from something or someone. I didn't pressure her too much, for I attuned in her own time, she'd come clean with me.

I waited and waited for her to confide in me, somehow. She didn't. I had to admit, it drove me into a certain indescribable cocoon of emotions. However, I also registered she just wanted that part of her life out of her memory. I respected that.

She was fiery, sexy, and wild. She moved like an adult. I never wanted to start a sexual relationship with her, but damn, Melanie was my Delilah. I got scared at some point, knowing perfectly well the consequences of my affair with an underage girl. Yet, I let my manly desires cloud my reasoning.

In as much as I loved the sex, I wanted to know her. I wanted to know what drove her out of Long Island. The obsession with learning about her past increased daily. It was so strong I had to resist calling Shae and seeking information from her.

I sighed as I clad in casual wear. A part of me knew she'd be back. Maybe it was wishful thinking, but I hoped it'd be true. I descended the stairs to the living room, only to see that the front door was left ajar.

“Melanie. Melanie.” I called out to her but came no response. I darted outside to the backyard. Still, there wasn't a sight of her. I couldn’t figure out why I searched for her. Common sense told me to let her go. After all, I gained nothing from her.

The sex, scumbag. An annoying ringing taunted in my head.

“Devante, have you by any chance seen Melanie?” I asked my next-door neighbor.

He shook his head in response. I waved at him and hopped into my car, dropping my phone onto the passenger's seat. I circled the entire neighborhood, praying I'd spot her. I hated how things ended between us. I hated having bad blood with people, especially ones I'd grown to care about. Yes, I cared about Melanie. It wasn't about the sex; it wasn't about her age. I just cared about her. Maybe it was the fact that, behind the white picket fences she exhibited, I saw the broken young woman she was. I didn't give her the benefit of the doubt. I was a scumbag to her. I should have told her about Daphne and my kids. Right now, I knew things would never go back to how it was, but I wanted to make things right.

After an hour of circling around the neighborhood to no avail, an idea popped into my head. I veered my car in the opposite direction, set my car in a speed motion, and drove to where I first met her. If she truly was headed back to Long Island, that was the one place she wouldn't miss. Luckily for me, the highway wasn't jammed in traffic. Throughout the entire drive there, I called her.

Not a single one did she pick.

It filled me with both rage and anxiety. Angry that I chased a minor like she bore my soul and anxious that something had happened to her.

In my tenth attempt to reach her, it went straight to voice mail.

“Melanie, please pick up your goddamn phone. I need to speak to you. We need to talk. I'm sorry for how things went down. Please call me or pick up.” I grunted and slammed my phone on the car seat. I only had one last turn till I reached that street. *Unity* Street.

In haste, I almost crashed into another car. The incident filled me with a crippling sense of Deja vu. My phone suddenly rang, and without warning, I slammed it onto my ears.

“What the hell is wrong with you?” I hissed at her.

“Uhh...Am I speaking to Jerome?” I cursed underneath my breath when Daphne's chirpy voice flowed into my ear.

“Uhh...honey.” I stuttered.

“Why haven't you been answering my calls?” She

asked, her voice sounding like a browbeaten child.

"Honey," I said through gritted teeth, trying so hard not to snap at her. "I've been busy."

"I know, but still. I called you earlier, and your assistant picked up. She didn't give you the message, did she?" She sighed. "I know you'd call if she had."

"No. What message?" I asked, halting my car in front of one shop and turning my head like a lizard.

"Georgie and Lily want to see their grandma. You need to come home this weekend so that we can all go as a family."

"Alright, honey, I'll be there," I said, slamming my hand across my face, wondering how Daphne would feel about my infidelity with Melanie.

RICK

Episode Three

It'd been three days since hell broke loose in my house. The tension that engulfed this living space was one I'd never encountered before. Shae barely looked at me. She barely talked to me. She didn't give me attitude, but you could hint something was incredibly off with her. My quest to get her talking was in vain. She wouldn't breathe out a word and always said everything was fine. There were times in my life I'd been uneasy and frustrated, but none came close to the silent treatment from Shae.

Over the days, I pondered Dennis' words. I was aware it was a great risk if I went through with his advice. But a part of me attuned to the fact. A part of me wondered if Shae waited for me to come clean to her.

I'd committed a grave sin against the one woman I loved. I betrayed her trust, and I knew I was selfish for discarding my transgression and acting like everything was alright when deep down it wasn't. The fear of losing her glued my mouth from confessing the truth, but if I were honest to myself, that same fear should have prevented me from hurting her in the first place.

Shae didn't even sleep in the same bed with me. She gave a flimsy excuse of being with Miranda at night since she cried a lot. She flinched when I touched her. The farthest we've gone in our intimacy was a perk on the lips. Every now and then, when I went out for lectures, I had a difficult time returning home and seeing those empty, shadowed eyes.

I jumped out of my bed, ventured towards the door, and peeked at Shae and Miranda in the living room. She was rocking Miranda while vacantly staring into the void. I shut the door, sighed, and went into my closet. I dug through my clothes, searching for my spare phone. The phone I'd buried almost three months ago. After several minutes of futile search, I felt sweat gather up my forehead. With my hands slumped on my hips, I calculated the possible areas I'd hidden this phone. Every bone in my body knew I hadn't disposed of it. I'd kept it in this very closet.

Rushing to the bed, I grabbed my other phone and called Dennis.

"Yo man, what's up." His raspy voice came at me, and for a split second, I wondered what he was up to.

"I can't find my phone." I let out an exasperated sigh.

"Oh..kay, dummy. How are you speaking to me then?" He asked in a conceiting tone as I perched at the edge of the bed.

"Not this one. You know, the other one." I said, rolling my eyes and imagining how stupid he looked now.

"You mean the one you were using to send those anonymous messages to Melanie, scaring her to leave town?" He asked.

"Yes, that one."

"Man, are you crazy? You don't keep your murder weapons with you after you use them in your crime. You dispose of them." He was shaking his head. I didn't need to see it. I knew Dennis way too much not to identify his reaction after every statement. “Did you at least delete the messages?”

“Yeah... no,” I whispered, slamming my hand across my face. I was in deep shit.

“Yo man, that's crazy. Are you sure you kept it in your closet? Maybe you've forgotten where you really kept it.”

“No, man, I'm dead ass positive I kept it in there.” The fan was set on the highest mark, but for some reason, I still felt hot.

“You asked Shae? I mean, she does your laundry and stuff.”

“Dude, she's been in this house for the longest time, and it’s been intact. Always in its hiding place when I look for it.”

“By the way, have you been able to tell her the truth? I meant to call you and ask about that, but I've been occupied lately. You know, with the semester about to end and shit.”

“Yeah, yeah, I understand. No man, I haven't told her no shit.”

"You know she's beginning to look suspicious. Ever since you told me about that drunken night."

"I know. I still don't know the damage I caused. I sighed. Footsteps neared the bedroom door. "Ohkay, man, I have to go. Later ai."

"Later, my man." The door opened, and I threw my phone on the bed. I couldn't put myself in any carefree position before Shae entered.

"Hey." She said, walking to her side of the closet.

"Hey," I replied, looking everywhere but her. She pulled out a bag and started packing her clothes in it. My heart hammered wildly in my chest as I lost the ability to speak. I only stared at her, watching what appeared to be a rebated yet determined move. She halted, jerked her head at me, and caught me staring.

"Miranda?" I foolishly let out.

She arched an eyebrow. "Asleep. Oh, I nearly forgot." She gasped, then went to where the mirror stood. She pulled one of the drawers opened and revealed my phone. The phone I nearly lost my mind over. "This out off your closet yesterday."

"Yesterday?" I checked the time, and it was 2pm. The urge to ask her which time she found it was unwavering yet stupid. Whichever time she saw it, she'd already discovered everything on it. This phone didn't even have a lock.

"Oh, okay. I was looking for it."

"Of course, you would." She smirked and sauntered to her original position. "So, Rick, you ready to come clean or not?"

I blinked at her as if she'd grown another head. Reality slapped me across the face as I instantly understood the saying *nothing stayed hidden under the sun*. "Shae. What are you talking about?"

She cackled and looked at me like a clown. "Oh really, you're going to do this. You're going to play dumb now? I went through that phone, Rick. I know everything going on. You better tell me the truth, or I'll leave. And oh heavens should hold me; this will be the last time you'd see me." Her eyes darkened, and I gulped. "And feel free to have Miranda to yourself. She's your daughter, isn't she?"

JERONE

<u>*Episode Four*</u>

I slammed my car door as I made my way to the car boot to yank out my suitcase. I threw my head to gaze at the duplex apartment before me. Before I dragged my suitcase through the picket fences, my children burst out of the front doors and embraced me. It'd been two weeks since I saw them. The last time I came home was the lie I told Melanie that I was going on a business trip. George was sick and needed to be sent to the hospital, and since he and I were tight buddies, I had to be there.

I knew what I did to Daphne wasn't fair. Our marriage was perfect. Well, perfect till I took a journey on the road of infidelity. She was the perfect mother and wife. She'd had my back from the *90s*. It was her unique personality that made me marry her. I knew there wouldn't be any woman who matched out to her. It'd break her heart once she got to learn of my infidelity. Knowing Daphne, she wouldn't mind taking all the kids away from me. She'd tell them the truth, and I wouldn't be able to bear the hatred from my own kids.

"I missed you, daddy," Lily said, clutching at my grey pantaloons. Lily was six while Georgie was ten.

"I miss you more, dad. See, I'm so much better now. I took all my medicine and didn't let mom nag." George chipped in.

"You know what," I said, bending to their level. "This evening, I'll take you both out for ice cream."

"Yayy." They cheered in unison, and my heart broke and soared at the same time. "Let's go to mommy. "

"Look who's home." Daphne emerged into the living room from the kitchen. She wore an apron over a blouse and jeans she wore. Her curly hair was up in a messy bun. Her mocha skin was even more flawless from when I last came home. The urge to rush to her and kiss her senseless was alarming, but when the thought of my infidelity sprung up in me, I hesitated.

“So, you're going to pretend you didn't hear my children screaming, daddy.”

“No.” She laughed, advanced towards me, and kissed me tenderly on the lip. She smelled like the chicken Alfredo she was making. Also one of my favorite dishes.

“You knew I'd be home, so you decided to make my favorite dish, isn't it?”

“Please, you’re just lucky.” She cupped my face in her hands. “I missed you, baby. You make it so hard for me to reach you when you're in Elmont.”

My heart thumped wildly in my chest as she mentioned Elmont. Melanie's image settled in my brain, and I had to shake my head before it disappeared. I'd spent the past couple of days searching for her, leaving her messages like a psychotic person. Well, it was done. I wasn't going to waste my time with her anymore.

“I promise I won't do that again.” I kissed her on the cheek before calling out to the kids.

“Why don't you go change. Dinner will be ready soon.” She said to me, and I nodded. I scrambled upstairs with the kids snuggling up against my legs like leeches.

This was one of the most doting affections from my kids and one I always missed.

It was great to be home.

***

"Look at how my grandkids have gotten so big. Daphne, you're doing one heck of a job." My father hugged both kids and gave Daphne a pleasing smile. We'd been at their house for the past fifteen minutes. I had to admit it'd been so long since I came to visit them.

"Oh really. You giving all the credit to Daphne now?" I feigned jealousy while pulling my wife into my arms.

"Don't be jealous, honey." She cackled.

"He should be. He's never around. Always away on a business trip. You're lucky, son. Daphne is a good woman. No woman will stay and take that crap." My father gestured with an index finger.

"I know I wouldn't." My mother added as she placed a bowl of French fries in front of the kids.

"When your mom and I got married, I had to transfer

from where I used to work and get a place closer to home. That's how you and your siblings turned out fine."

"Don't you miss your father when he's away, my dears?" My mom asked them.

"We do, momma," George replied, shoving a French fry into his mouth.

"Reconsider, son. Family is worth more than making money. You and wife Daphne have a comfortable life." She added.

They were right. I didn't like this subject because they were right. Three months ago, the CEO accepted my request to transfer to the sub-divisional company which was located here, at home. Meeting Melanie changed everything. And judging from my intuition, I didn't know where I stood now. I could always go back for the transfer, but was it something I wanted? A part of me wasn't ready to entirely cut Melanie from my life. But when I stared at the people seated behind the glass table, I knew I had to make a decision. Daphne grasped my hand tightly, and I gave her a smile. My mom and dad gave me the same *you can do better* look. While Lily and George focused on nothing but the food in front of them.

"You know Lily and George are still young. We have a long way to go in funding their education". I reasoned.

"Son, even if you make a million dollars for them, no happiness will ever come close to having you there with them. Your mom and I always argue on a lot of things, but the one thing I never questioned her on was when she told me to take a job closer to home." My dad added.

Daphne was quiet, and you could tell a lot ran through her mind.

"So, think about it, the money you're making or building a stronger relationship with your family. Which is more significant."

I nodded at them. My answer wasn't in the options he listed out.

RICK

Episode Five

"Miranda is your daughter, isn't she?" She asked in a trembling voice. All the blood from my body flowed to the floor. My knuckles were nippy, and my body turned incredibly pale for a black man. I glanced over my shoulder to peer at her, and my heart shattered into pieces. The only secret I had sworn to take to my grave had magically popped out like daises in the snow. Now, I had to bear the consequences of my actions. It was nothing but a mistake. How was I going to explain to Shae everything that happened was a mistake?

"Answer me, Rick. Cat's got your tongue?"

"Shae." I let out, slowly standing to my feet and taking baby steps towards her. The plan was to remain transfixed at arm's reach. "I'm sorry. I can explain."

"Explain what, Rick. That you were fucking my best friend behind my back. How could you be so cruel? I thought you loved me." She bellowed out, and not even once did I try to stop her. She had every right to storm at me that way.

"It's not like that, I promise you." I leaned closer, looking intently at her and then breaking contact after two seconds.

She let out a nasty cackle and held her hand to me, making me halt. "So, what is it like? You weren't fucking Melanie? Miranda isn't your daughter? Cos I've gathered every proof, and you can't lie when there's evidence, Rick. You can't lie about shit like this."

I thought of the right things to say, but none came. There wasn't any way I could sugar- coat what I did. It became clear that I'd lost Shae. It didn't matter whether I told her the truth or not. "You're right. Miranda is my daughter, but I wasn't sleeping with Melanie. It was a one- time thing. You have to believe me." The news broke her. She wiped the tears from her eyes, and I knew

I didn't want to feel what she felt at that moment.

"One-time thing? Was it on last year, Halloween night?" She said, and I blinked rapidly at her. That piece of information wasn't included in the texts. How did she know that? Unless_

"You're wondering how I found out that you fucked my best friend on that night, right?" She chuckled amidst the tears and hurled her suitcase across the floor. My heart skipped, instantly getting terrified. "How could you do this to me?"

"I never wanted to, Shae. I was drunk. We were both drunk. I... It's...." I stuttered, overwhelmed that I'd come to this. I wasn't a cheater. I never cheated in any of my relationships before Shae, so it hurt- it was devastating that I'd come to this.

"Don't tell me that crap, Rick. It only makes your betrayal worse. You knew what you were doing. It doesn't matter if you were drunk. You knew. You knew afterward. You knew she was pregnant for an entire nine months. You knew, but you decided to keep it away from me. So, don't try that flimsy excuse on me." She pointed her index finger at me as her darkened eyes bore into mine. "You know, everything makes sense now. The reason_" Miranda's shrilling voice resonated into the bedroom, and I let out an exasperated sigh. "The reason you wanted me to stay wasn't that you loved me. You needed someone to play mom to your child."

"I'm sorry, Shae."

"And you chased Melanie out of town with your anonymous threats. Why?"

"Cos I was scared she'd tell you the truth eventually." I exhaled. I discerned I only made my situation worse with my stupid mumbling. “I didn't want you to find out because I was afraid to lose you.”

"Well, I have found out. You couldn't have hidden it forever, Rick. Guess what, you have lost me too."

"Shae, no. Please, I love you." I caught her by the hand, but she shoved me away fiercely.

"No, don't tell me that bullshit. You don't love me, Rick. If you did, you wouldn't hurt me the way you have. You wouldn't. So, don't stand there talking to me about love. When your actions perfectly contradicted it."

"Don't leave Shae. Let's work through this. Please, I can't lose you. I can't bear it. Everything I did was to prevent a raging aftermath like this one."

"I am leaving." She wiped the tears with the back of her hand and proceeded to yank her clothes into her suitcase. Miranda's tears wailed once more, and I wondered if she'd been continuously crying from the first time. "You can attend to your daughter now. If you're lucky, Melanie will come home, and you can be a happy family. And oh, I bet your mother will like her."

"No, Shae. Don't go."

"If you come near me, you wouldn't like what I'll do next." She said in a ravenous voice, lunged her suitcase to the floor, and just like that, I watched her leave and slam the door shut.

Defeated, crushed, and wounded were among what I felt. I sank to the floor, face buried in my hands, tears gushing out like a baby. I'd just lost the love of my life, and I knew Shae. She wouldn't take me back. Before we got together, she made me understand how cheating was an absolute deal-breaker for her. I promised her to never hurt her that way, and it was exactly what I did.

Heavens knew it was going to take a miracle for even a conversation to spring up between us. But with her gone, all I had left was Miranda. Truth was, I was clueless about how to go about things with her. I only became a good parent because she guided me.

As I struggled to get back on my feet, the ambiance of the room- the entire apartment changed. The vibrant colors and texture that splashed across the room were replaced with a dull, bleak greyness.

The elusive energy Shae brought was gone, and it was never coming back.

JEROME

Episode Six

It'd been a week since I came home to my family, and I must say, the peace that engulfed me was one I had never experienced. Truly, there was no place like home. Every day was a fun day for my kids and me. The hollow space that was created in all the weeks I was away from them filled each passing day. The light that sparked in their eyes every morning at my sight, the joy of me driving them to school. All these and more almost made me remember how fun parenting was while I was away. I pondered over my parents' words a great deal. Whether I should stay or I should go. I didn't want to break my family's heart, especially Daphne. She certainly was the purest of all humans. I'd been going to and fro, and never once did she question me about my fidelity. Sometimes, I feared she knew but buried the argument for the sake of our kids.

My intuition screamed I confess everything about Melanie. Maybe that would be the remedy to the dreams and night terrors I had of her. Not once did I understand the real meaning behind these dreams. Not once did I fathom why I had those dreams. I wasn't a superstitious individual, yet I couldn't help but wonder if something terrible had happened to her. These dreams would keep me up until Daphne spotted me in the kitchen and carried me back to sleep. Of course, she never stopped questioning me about what the problem was and I, clearly in my right senses, wasn't ready to blast this information to her.

Instead, I stopped thinking about it and devised other ways to tackle this new battle of mine.

"Will daddy pick us up from school today?" Lily asked as her mother helped put her bag on. Daphne glanced over her shoulder at me and wrinkled her eyebrows at me.

"Yes, honey, he would. You know daddy loves to do

stuff with you." She said in a playful tone, cupping both their cheeks in her hands. It was a lovely sight. Definitely, something I'd love to witness every day.

An hour later, the only person left in the house was me. For the past week, I'd been home, and I worked from my laptop. I spent a few hours behind my laptop, got the necessary work done, and idled the rest of the hours in utter nonsense.

In one of my ideas to combat Melanie's issue, her friend, Shae, was the first person to come to mind. For some reason, I never believed Melanie's version of the story she told me about Shae. It was easier to see through people's emotions but even easier to read them vividly when they were standing two feet from you. I hurdled my phone out of my bag and scrolled through my contacts. I recalled saving her number, but difficult being sure since the only time we spoke was when she called Melanie's phone.

"Bingo." I cheered and called her.

"Hello," I said when she picked up. "Am I speaking to Shae?"

"Yeah." She sounded a bit off or simply uninterested in anything I had to say.

"This is Jerome. I don't know if you'd remember me, but I picked up the phone when you called Melanie sometime ago."

"Oh, okay, what do you want?" I arched an eyebrow, a tad bit surprised at her rude response, but I gave her the benefit of the doubt, taking how nice she was when we spoke the first time.

"The thing is, we had an argument, and she left." "She told me she was returning to Long Island."

"Oh really? She's coming back here. Interesting." She said in a rather slurry tone. "Yes. I...I understand you're friends."

"No, we're not friends." She spat out like venom.

"Okay. Sisters?" I tried again. There was no way Melanie's story about them was true. She cackled, and I blew out a frustrated sigh.

"Okay, Shae. That's not the point. The point is I want to find her."

"You're in love with her." The words came out of her

mouth, and I wasn't really sure if it was a question or a statement.

"No," I whispered. "I just need to settle some bad blood between us."

"Well, I can't help you. If she claimed she was returning to Long Island, then it's either she hasn't arrived, or she's hiding under a rock. Either way, I can't help you. I have to go_."

"Please, you really need to help me find her."

"I don't want anything to do with that traitor. If you're bent on fixing this bad blood you have with her, that's your problem."

"How about I come to Long Island, and we find her together?" I said, and the line went silent. "It's obvious you also have some unfinished business with her. Think about it. We can both benefit from this search party."

"I'm not interested in....confronting her. She's not worth it. They're not worth it. In fact, you also aren't worth it. So, if you'd please excuse me. I have to go back to my sorrowful life." She clicked her teeth which made me smile.

"I'm coming to Long Island. To find you first and then Melanie."

"If you insist. Just know that she's not worth it. She's not worth the effort, time, and money you're about to waste. And if you're in love with her, you chose the wrong person to love." I wouldn't have taken her seriously if not for the solemnity in her voice. As the line went dead, I couldn't help but wonder what skeletons Melanie had in her closest. Was everything Shae said true?

I pushed the thoughts down, knowing in less than 48 hours, I would get all the answers I wanted. The next probing thing to tackle was my family. Once again, I was about to destroy the uplifting aura in the house.

I had to find a way to prevent that from happening but also find a way to leave for Long Island.

RICK

Episode Seven

"Yo, man, we need to finish this assignment ASAP. We can't have you zoning out every time." Dennis' strong hands hit the table and broke me out of my trance. I blinked hard and slammed my hand across my face. I was beginning to lose my mind. Everywhere I turned, I saw Shae. Her eyes, her laugh, her smile, her tears, and her anger. I saw everything, and it gradually drew me insane. "I know you're in a hard place right now, but this assignment is important too."

"Yeah, you're right, man. I'm sorry. Let's do it." Twenty minutes of effective work passed before I zoned out again. My mind drifted to the years I'd been with Shae- and how everything had come tumbling down.

I'd always had this gut feeling that slipped some hope in me when I faced some challenges. Unfortunately for me, I had no assurance or hope this time. Unbeknownst to me, my head was on the table, and I only felt the sharp nudge from Dennis.

I lifted my head and discerned the frown on his face. "Okay, let's take some break. You clearly need it. So, Shae found out, and she's left. It happens. I don't mean to sound insensitive, but you're not the first man that something like this has happened to."

"I know, Dennis. I really don't need a pep talk." I sighed.

"I'm not giving you one. You just need to prove to her you're really sorry. Show up at her house and workplace. Everywhere, every time. How many days has it been since she moved out?"

"Three days," I said with a nod. Those three days felt like an eon of years-especially the nights. I spent every night thinking about her. I spent the nights missing her so badly. I yearned for her.

"Wow. And have you made any attempts to see her?

You know, trying to apologize?" I shook my head no, and he rolled his eyes at me. "And how's Miranda?"

"I hired a nanny. She's currently at home with her." I didn't know if it was just me, but the cafeteria suddenly turned irritable to me, and I needed to vamoose out of here. "You don't get it, do you? I don't think she'll ever take me back, Dennis."

"She might. You just have to show her how sorry you are. You never stop showing it until she forgives you."

"What if she forgives me but won't take me back?"

He shrugged. "There's always the possibility of that. But right now, if I'm being completely honest with you, you should focus on gaining her forgiveness rather than wanting her back. What you did is forgivable but unacceptable, and it's going to take a lot of work to get a woman like Shae back."

"You know what kills me? The thought of someone else having her." I gritted my teeth in sheer agony and stomped to my feet. "I'm going to see her. I've been having sleepless nights, and I don't think I'll ever return to my rational self until she forgives me."

"Dude, we're in the middle of a very important assignment."

I stared at him in disbelief, thought it wise to not say a word, and scampered out of the cafeteria. I didn't know where to go first- either to her house or her workplace. The cafeteria was closer to her house, so I made it my first area of contact.

At a warping speed, I arrived in just a few minutes. The environment was serene, and it didn't appear like she was around. I jerked out of my car and darted to the entrance, my heartbeat the only repetitive sound I could hear.

"Shae," I said while simultaneously pounding on the door. There came no response, and I turned the doorknob. It was closed. For minutes, I knocked on the door, thinking if she was in there, she couldn't hide forever.

"She's not around." A coarse voice said from behind me. I spun, and my eyes fell on an older-looking man. I tried recalling his name as Shae had mentioned him to me before but to no avail. "If you want to see her so badly, you can go to her job" He offered and took off.

I muttered a thank you to him and bounced into my car. I'd been to Shae's job a couple of times, so locating it wasn't a hurdle. I parked my car behind a truck- rest assured I wouldn't be handed a ticket. Thankfully for me, I gained easy access as the security guards who were supposed to stand guard at the door were involved in banter with two heavily tattooed men. I sauntered into the club, and there weren't a lot of people in there. With the time being only 11 am, I perfectly understood.

I walked to the bartender and asked for Shae. He looked at me squarely before gesturing to a door on his left. "It's the only door with a label on it." He said, wiping the insides of a glass with a napkin.

Muttering a note of appreciation, I darted towards the door. Unsure whether to knock or just enter, I went with the latter and slowly opened the door and crept in. Luckily for me, there weren't any naked ladies in there- there wasn't any lady at all. As I twirled the little space, looking for anything that could serve as an indication, another door opened.

"What are you doing here?" Shae emerged, rigged in her uniform.

I swallowed a huge bubble of air and ventured toward her. "Shae, can I see you for a few minutes? I need to talk to you."

"I'd rather walk in a sea of crocodiles than spend a second with you. Get out before I call security." She said with a death glare and an unwavering tone.

Involuntarily, I swallowed another gulp of air and felt a sharp pain in my heart.

JEROME

Episode Eight

Convincing my family this was the last business trip I'd take was a galumph move. The kids weren't afraid to show how unhappy they were. They only smiled when I took them out for ice cream- a smile that stretched on one side of the lip. Daphne, on the other hand, didn't speak to me. The conversation that ensued between us almost made me rethink my decision. But just as I promised- this was going to be the last time I went on any trip.

Shae had already cautioned me not to come. She wasn't going to make herself available. She had no information about Melanie and wasn't interested in knowing anything about her. Regardless, I'd tuned my mind to embark on this quest. Despite her negative response to me meeting her, after much plea and convincing, Shae gave me her address. I had only one motive. Hear what Shae had to say about Melanie. For some reason, I felt like a detective investigating a case- I was investigating a case, the case of Melanie and her mysterious disappearance.

My car came to a halt when I reached Shae's home address. Her house was rather tiny. Not what I expected. I slammed the car door shut and marched towards the entrance. It was a quaint neighborhood- so much better than in Elmont. I pressed a knock on her door and waited for several seconds. When no response came, I knocked again, retrieving my phone from my pocket to call her just in case. Creaking sounds came from behind the door. Less than a minute, the door opened to reveal Shae.

Unlike Melanie with straight permed hair, Shae was in braids that were tied in a messy bun. She had soft features and could easily be discerned as a teenager, unlike Melanie, who possessed mature lineaments. Her face was puffy, and underneath her eyes were obvious dark circles. Even though we'd never met before, I instantly knew she wasn't in the best mental state. She folded her arms and looked at me with no readable expression. "Yes, who are you?"

"You're Shae, right?" I asked, only to receive no reply. Clearing my throat to hide my embarrassment, I gave her an assuring smile. "I'm Jerome."

She flashed her eyes in astonishment. "So, you really did come? Do you like her? Or you're in love with her." If I perused the expression on her eyes, there was a hint of contempt in them.

"Neither of what you mentioned. I already told you I feel bad for how things ended with us, so I just want to make amends." She looked everywhere but my face as she stepped away from the door.

"I'd invite you in, but I don't have any couches or those fancy stuff. We can sit here." She pointed to two chairs in the corridor. "You're married?" I saw her eyes settle on my hand.

"Yes, I am," I said, slumping to the other chair facing her.

"Did you fuck Melanie?"

It was my turn to be surprised at her question. In my judgement, I felt a little disrespected she asked that. Another part of me also wanted to know the reason she asked that. I opened my mouth to answer but changed my mind? "Did I fuck- sleep with Melanie?" I tried to reiterate as possible as I could.

"Don't worry, I won't judge. I mean, I wouldn't be surprised if you two have. She seems to possess some charm that sends all men bazookas. You- you look like a victim. So, your lack of response tells me you've fucked her. Now, what do you want to know? She's not here. I haven't seen her in the past five months or so."

"What was your relationship with her? I want the honest answer, Shae."

She sighed, then rubbed her eyes. "We used to be best friends. Wherever she is, she probably still thinks we are, but we're not. You know the reason she left Long Island?"

"She told me you betrayed her," I said without thinking and instantly regretted it.

"I betrayed her?" She gave me a puzzled look and smirked. "She's the traitor. She fucked my boyfriend behind my back." The disdain that seethed from her voice gave me chills. I watched her shut her eyes for what seemed like an eternity. I knew it was a ploy to prevent tears from coming. "And you know-" She choked, "-You know the worst part is that they had a baby. They have a baby together." Her eyes closed again. "God, this hurts so much. I loved Miranda so much that when she left, I was willing to take up motherly roles for her, not knowing__."

"Are you still with your boyfriend?" Not the best question to have come out that moment, but I still processed the bombshell information about Melanie in my head. I understood the hurt Shae felt. She lied and betrayed her own best friend. I should be happy the only foul she committed with me was lying about her life.

"No. I ended things with him the minute I found out." She sniffed and wiped her nose with the back of her hand.

"I still don't understand why she left Long Island. I

don't think it was before you found out?"

"No, she left because my boyfriend, apparently, was sending her threatening messages to expose her if she didn't leave town. I guess that's what scared her and drove her to leave. So, how did you meet her?"

"I almost hit her with my car. She appeared lifeless-like she didn't care whether she lived or died. I guess her vulnerability was what drew me to her. I asked her to get in my car. We had a short conversation where she told me how miserable life was. I only took her in cos I feared for her. You get it?"

"And you ended up sleeping with her. You men are all the same. You're all fucking cheaters." She scoffed. "Well, that's all I can tell you about Melanie. Now, if you'd excuse me, I'd like to go back inside."

Before I could say another word, her door was slammed shut. *Wow, she must really hate me.* I blew out a breath and dug my phone out. I dialed Melanie's number and stuck it onto my phone. My heart raced when it went through, then the beep came, signaling she'd picked.

"Hello, Jerome."

"Melanie?"

RICK

Episode Nine

"I'm serious, Rick. Don't make me repeat myself." She exhaled sharply, balling her fist yet never bearing me one eye contact. Instead, she closed her eyes as if disgusted by my sight. And why wouldn't she? I was disgusted with myself.

"Shae, I know you don't want to see me. But please, just spare me a minute." I pleaded, clasping my hands together and fighting the urge to not cry. I took one step toward her. She stepped backward, making her back crash against the table behind her. She winced softly, sighed, and folded her arms.

"What do you want, Rick? Are you here to torment me some more?" Her voice broke as she spoke.

"No. You have no idea the boldness I had to gather

before coming here. I know you hate me, and you have every right to. But I want you to believe me when I say I'm sorry. I didn't mean to hurt you. I was drunk."

"That's not an excuse. And why are we having this conversation again, Rick." Another sigh escaped her as her fingers brushed over her eyes. This was when I noticed how hollow her eyes looked. She'd lost weight, and I wondered how I didn't notice this before. "You know what, Rick, it doesn't matter. The harms already been done. If you want an answer as to whether I forgive you. Yes, I do. But I don't think we can be together again. I can't, knowing that you and my best friend have a daughter together. I just.... I just can't." The tears she tried so hard not to shed fell like a waterfall. "You need to leave now, and please, if you love me as you claim, you'd leave me the hell alone."

"Shae," I whispered. What she asked me was the hardest thing anyone had to tell me. It was a compromise I couldn't go through with.

"Please." This time, she did look at me- in the eye. "Leave, or this time I will call security. For what's worth,

I heard Melanie is in town. You two can be a family with Miranda." With a weak smile, she grabbed a white napkin from the table and disappeared through the same door she emerged from.

Biting the sides of my cheeks to not cry, I rushed out of the club and into my car. With no direction in mind, I just drove. Drove like a mad man. I didn't care if I crashed or not. I didn't care whatever happened. Like a spontaneous move, the car halted in front of a pub. With my hands firmly pressed on the steering wheel, I stared at the entrance of the pub. Using alcohol to forget your problems was a move I regarded as cowardice. Yet somehow, I didn't care if I was being a coward. I darted out of my car and straight into the pub.

I marched straight to the bartender and requested the strongest alcohol they had. After just seven shots, a twinge of outrageous confidence swiveled through me. With my deflated cognition at work, I walked to a couple who appeared all lovey-dovey at one of the booths. I stretched out a hand in a request for a dance. The man who was bigger and so much taller than me squared an eye at me. I didn't blink, for the confidence I had at that moment could make me stand up to anyone.

"Oh, c'mon, baby. It's just a dance." The lady, who was either a red-head or brunette, said to him. She got up and took my hand. I saluted the man, and with a hand on the lady's hip, we strode to the dance floor. The music played here wasn't like the ones played in the club, yet it was chill enough to vibe with. She moved with grace, every hip sway reminding me of Shae. The way she pumped to the music. She was just too full of life. I blinked as it occurred to me; I described Shae instead of this woman here. Under the facsimile neon lights and twirling of her hair, I did see Shae. It was her. It had to be.

I grabbed Shae's hand, tugged her closer to me, and kissed her. I scrunched my face at how different her lips tasted. Shae always tasted like strawberry since she used a strawberry-scented gloss. This taste was, however, like vodka. I coughed, and before I raised my head, a slap fell across my face. I touched my face and shut my eyes for what seemed like infinity.

"How dare you?" She shrieked and skipped past me faster than Flash. I blinked hard in an attempt to gain consciousness.

A rough nudge came on my shoulder. The minute I spun, a punch was gifted to my face. I winced in pain, losing my balance and falling flat on my face. My vision became dazed as a trickle of blood sipped into my mouth. I struggled to get up, but the macho man had already tugged at my shirt.

"Keep your filthy mouth off of my girlfriend. Or you're going to get in some nasty trouble, you bastard." He spat in my face and threw another punch at me before scampering away. By now, one of my eyes had shut completely. I couldn't even open it if I tried. In my blurred vision, I saw two men exit the macho man and his girlfriend. With every strength I had left, I got on my feet and walked into the bathroom. Cleaning myself, it felt like a thousand needles were nuzzled into my face.

I scurried out of the bathroom, still in pain from my bloody nose and black eye. I grabbed my phone and texted Dennis. I wasn't in the condition to drive, and although I did feel like dying, I'd gotten enough beating for the day.

Thirty minutes passed, and while Dennis hadn't arrived, I resorted to more alcohol shots, repelled at how pathetic I'd become. I felt a tap on my back- too soft a tap coming from a guy. I turned, and my heart did a million flips.

"Shae. You're here. Why are you here?" I slurred, my fingers gesturing across her face, my own way of calming the jitters in my stomach.

She didn't say a word, yet her face held so many expressions. Disappointment being the most transparent of them. She flashed her phone across my face. "You texted me, asshole."

"Shit," I muttered under my breath and checked my phone to see the honest yet stupid mistake I'd made.

JEROME

Episode Ten

"What happened to you, Melanie? Where are you?" I asked like I was her protective yet overly possessive boyfriend. I wasn't. I was her friend. For some reason, I grimaced at the thought of Melanie and I being friends. This was the second time I had called her. And I couldn't hide the surprise when she picked up. The first time at Shae's house, she hung up after she passed a rather snarky response.

"What's your problem, Jerome? For such an insensitive asshole, I didn't think you had a heart. So, tell me why you've been blowing up my phone?" Her voice was harsh, and I asked myself if I deserved it this time. The first time, I accepted it but now?

"Where are you? Are you in Long Island?" I parked

my car at a nearby gas station. After my encounter with Shae, my next destination was home. I intended on leaving yesterday after we spoke. That was my plan until Melanie finally answered, changing the course of everything- again.

"Yes, I am. I've been here for the past two weeks. I told you I was coming here. You think I was bluffing. You're really an asshole for saying all those things you said back there. And then you've been calling my phone since." She said in that same harsh tone, and I attuned she wouldn't hesitate to throw something- anything at me if I was standing within a close range of her.

"So, where exactly are you?" It was rather peculiar that I asked for her exact address, yet she had no idea I was also in Long Island. She gave a sarcastic comment before spilling it out. "Oh, okay. Are you happy, though? I mean, okay. Are you okay?"

"Do you care?" She spat out, and I could imagine her smirking.

"You know what, never mind. Have a good life. Melanie." I said with a subtle smile. We hung up, and

I pumped my fist. Searching her motel on my Google map, I swerved my car in the opposite direction. Since I wasn't familiar with the roads and streets of Long Island, finding Melanie's motel was like solving rocket science. The only thing that kept me calm through the one-hour drive was the curated road trip playlist that played.

"Yes." I cheered when I arrived at the motel. It was the ugliest building I'd seen, and that was coming from someone who once lived in the projects. The paint was worn off, and the cracks on the walls were so visible and deep. It looked like it'd collapse any second. There were weeds sprouting on every soiled part of the ground. Simply put, this building was a fixer-upper and unfit to be rented out to anyone. Maybe animals, but not people. Why on earth would Melanie settle in a rat hole like this?

I made my way to the entrance, and my eyes fell on the receptionist, who chewed gum noisily and had his legs swinging over the desk. I deliberately tapped my feet noisily on the dirty tiled floor. He didn't even raise an eyebrow to acknowledge my presence. I sighed inwardly, marching closer to him, but he halted me with a gesture of his finger.

"Hi, I'm looking for Melanie_" I realized I didn't know her surname.

"Room 3A1." He said, face buried in his phone. With a nod of appreciation, I trudged to the said room. It was on the second floor, and I could swear every step on the stair made it creak. It was only a matter of time before it collapsed. Reaching the designated door, I knocked on it.

It took a while for her to respond and when she finally did- oh- the disbelief on her face was one I could live for. Her eyes bulged open, and she blinked like she'd instantly lost her mind. "What are you doing here?"

"Surprise. Surprise, Melanie. Mind letting me in? We have lots of catching up to do."

"What are you doing in Long Island?" It was so easier to see how pissed she was at my sight. How her chest heaved, and nostrils flared, I knew she wanted to pounce on me. "Are you that obsessed with me,

Jerome?"

"I came to see Shae." Of course, that was a mere statement to see how she'd react, and yes, I noticed the fear in her eyes.

"You're bluffing." She let out a weak chuckle, a failed attempt to mask her uneasiness.

"I did. I'm not." I wanted to tell her I knew everything about her. The lies, the betrayal, everything. Yet that could possibly mean another escape plan from her. So, I kept my cool. "She misses you."

"What else did she tell you?" The vein in her neck bulged, and I sensed fear. More fear.

"Nothing." I shrugged. "To be honest, Melanie. I didn't come here to see Shae. I came to find you. I've been looking for you for so long." I rubbed my hand through my hair, took a deep breath, and looked at her, hoping she'd buy the story I sold to her. At that moment, I saw the minor I had sex with- I shamelessly took advantage of and knew I needed to ask for forgiveness. It was the only way I could start over with Daphne- my kids. "I didn't like how things ended with us. I shouldn't have said all those things to you. You shouldn't have lied to me about your age."

"Would that have changed anything?" She asked with a smug, leaning closer. She settled her arms around my neck, and I swallowed. "You really mean what you're saying, Jerome?" I nodded. "Okay, lemme ask you something. Do you regret what happened between us?"

I shut my eyes and opened them with a darkened look. She immediately withdrew her hand. "I do. You're a minor. I shouldn't have done that with you. I only came to ask your forgiveness."

"Well, I don't forgive you. I'm not going to give you closure. And I'm certainly not going to be your prop so you could feel better and return to your family. You lied to me too. You didn't tell me you had a wife or kids. So, we're both no angels. We belong together, don't you think?" She cackled like the wicked witch of the west.

"No. We don't. Go home to the people who love you. I'm going home to mine. I don't think you'll ever see me again." I said and turned my heel to leave. She didn't make a move to stop me. Quite frankly, I was glad she didn't. Once outside the building, I dialed Shae's number.

"Hey, Shae, you won't believe this. Melanie is in town. I just saw her."

RICK

Episode Eleven

Miranda's unpleasant wailings found way into my ears. I squeezed my closed eyes tightly as the sounds fairly increased. Convinced her shrills wasn't a dream, I fluttered my one good eye open. First thing I realized was I wasn't in my bed. A figure hovered over Miranda's crib, and I struggled to gain a full glance of the person. Could be Amelia. After all, she was Miranda's nanny. A wave of headache slammed in, and memory of what ensued previously replayed in my head. Miranda's crying only made my headache worse. I jolted up from the couch and rubbed my eye -like that would ease the avalanche of a headache in me.

"You're finally up." The voice didn't belong to Amelia. Even if I was dead, I could always recognize that voice.

Shae. "Here you go." My head hadn't gone up to hers. I simply snatched the glass of water from her and consumed everything in a single gulp. "There's some aspirin over there, but you had to finish the water first." She said, the sounds of her footsteps fading away as she disappeared.

"Thanks." There was more I wanted to say, but the fear of saying the wrong thing made me shut up. I downed the aspirin and sighed at yet another stupid mistake I had made. I recalled the events that brought Shae into my apartment. In my inebriated, beat-up state, I texted her rather. I had no idea how I could make such a mistake. A part of me wanted to owe it to fate. And that wishful thinking made me overthink the entire situation. Shae came up all the way to get me at the pub just because I texted her. The wishful thinking made me believe it was because she still cared about me. I could never forget the words she uttered at the club. It was as if a dagger had pierced through my heart. Seeing her now with the same unreadable expression splashed wildly on her face made my heart hammer. How could she be so indifferent toward me? How was it so easy for her?

Common sense told me I felt the way I did since I did her wrong. I was the dummy who let a gem slip, and so I had to endure the consequence. “Shae.” I gathered confidence and whispered her name. It took approximately five seconds for me to throw my head up and look at her. One hand rocked Miranda's crib while the other swung freely around her. “I... I'm sorry that you had to see me like this. And I'm sorry for texting you. I swear it was a mistake.” The last thing I needed her to think was that my desperate ass deliberately texted her.

“I know it was a mistake.” She said, blowing out a breath. Miranda had stopped crying, so she took a seat on the couch- a very wide interval between us.

“Why did you come?” I asked.

She smirked, then clapped her hands together. “There are only a few times you see Rick drunk. I knew you needed help. I discerned straight away you weren't sober. What I didn't expect, however, was the bloody nose and black eye. What happened?"

The sudden mentioning of those bolted the pain from the wounds again. My black eye instantly hurt, but I experienced no pain from my nose. "I... ugh... got into a... fight with someone. It was a stupid misunderstanding." If it weren't for the security guards, the macho man would have used me for some barbecue.

"Obviously, it was a fight. I'm asking the reason that led to it." Her voice was gentle. It was like her voice literally touched me. I recalled when her voice spoke to me that way. We both could be on the bed, having a very deep conversation. It could be her motivating me in any challenge I faced at that moment.

"I... it's stupid." I blinked, unable to look at her. I couldn't tell her I got beat up because I kissed someone that reminded me of her.

"Alright. Well, I sensed trouble, and I came. There was an older woman here. I didn't know you got Miranda a nanny."

"I can't do what you did with her." I gave her a weak smile.

"Yeah, I understand. She's a handful. But you're doing well. You're taking responsibility for her. Not everyone would do what you're doing." She sounded like she meant it, and it broke my heart into a thousand pieces.

"You were a very good mother to her," I said, jumping to my feet and moving to her crib. Mainly because I didn't want to see the expression that settled on her face after I said that.

"Melanie is here. She's staying at a motel." She cleared her throat.

"Oh, okay." Initially, if I heard that statement, my heart would explode. The blood in my body would vanish. With Shae discovering the truth, I didn't care. I didn't care if Melanie returned or not.

She kept silent but transfixed, a firm stare on my face. I knew she wanted to survey my features and peruse if I was uneasy. She broke contact after a few seconds and bit her lips. "Miranda will finally have both parents at her disposal. That's a good thing."

"I don't love her, Shae," I said through the pain that etched at the back of my throat. "She's not the one I want to be with."

"I'm not talking about that, Rick. I'm only referring to Miranda. I know the effects of broken homes. For a while, I wondered what story I'd tell Miranda when the time was right for her to know the truth. All her life, she'd have believed we were the biological parents. And I know it'd have broken her heart to learn we aren't. But now she has both mom and dad. She gets to be a happy child."

"Yeah, I'll do everything in my power for Miranda, but that's the closest relationship Melanie and I will ever have."

"I know Melanie, and I know you. You said you were drunk, but I know Melanie wasn't. She wanted what happened between the two of you. She wanted you, Rick. If she didn't, she wouldn't have had the baby." She sighed. "Melanie loves you. And you can learn to love her too."

Yet another gut-wrenching statement from her.

JEROME

Episode Twelve

It'd been two days since I returned from Long Island. The weight that bore on my shoulders previously had lifted and surprisingly been replaced with a new weight. The weight of coming clean about my infidelity to Daphne. I'd known Daphne for fifteen years now, and I'd be a fool to think she wouldn't leave so easily despite the number of years we'd been together. Heck, the woman wouldn't even stay for the kids as most women do. The thought of her leaving pushed me from telling her the truth, yet Shae somehow found way into my head. Her reaction after she discovered her boyfriend's infidelity.

A part of me told me I would prevent the deeper slash of betrayal and hurt if I came clean. This was the only skeleton in my closet, and the sooner I got rid of it, the better. I heaved a deep breath as I jumped up from the couch. I had only an hour to decide what to do. An hour before Daphne and the kids came home. An hour to make a decision that would completely change my life.

My phone rang, and I scoffed when I realized it was on the dining table. Truth be told, I wasn't in the mood for anyone. My only concern was Daphne, my kids, and, oh yeah, my parents. Daphne wouldn't hesitate to breathe a word to them of my infidelity. My features morphed from angst to warmth when I saw the caller ID.

"Good afternoon, Boss. It's a pleasure finally hearing from you." I knew the purpose of this call. With my current state of mind, I wished I hadn't requested the transfer from Elmont to home.

"Yes, Jerome. I saw your request letter two days ago. You want to be transferred back to New Jersey? Why? What happened in Elmont? The living conditions didn't favor you?" He asked.

"No, sir. None of that. But the truth is I've been away from my family for so long. I think I'm missing out on what parenting really is. I want to be around them. Work and come home to them every day." My voice sounded so convincing that I believed myself. Yet, I wished he saw within me and discerned the charade I put across.

"I understand, Jerome. Luckily for you, you're one of our best workers here in this company. I'll see what I can do, but do expect a positive response from me within this week."

"Thank you, sir." He hadn't yet made a decision. I didn't know whether to take that as a sign or an answer to my prayer. "I'll be expecting your call then," I said, and we hung up.

The minute the call ended, my ordeal resurfaced, and I slumped on the couch, burrowing my body into it. Heavens knew I hated lying. I wasn't a good liar. I wasn't the kind of person who took secrets to the grave. Until I came clean, I'd never be at peace.

So that was it. I had to confess to Daphne. And whatever decision she chose, I'd respect that.

The hour arrived quicker than Superman on a

mission. The horn from Daphne's car blew from the outside, signaling their arrival. With a happy face I'd been practicing for the past forty minutes, I sauntered out to the porch to welcome my family. If I focused on how elated they were to see me, the joy on Daphne's face as she came up to me and gave me a kiss, I'd choose this contented image and continue burying the darkness behind it.

"How was your day?" We were in the bedroom now. She changed from her formal uniform to a more casual, homey wear. She turned to smile at me, tiptoeing her way to me, and folded her arms around my neck. "I could get used to this, you know. Coming home and seeing you. Though, I know it's not always going to be like this when you start working. By the way, has your boss received the request and what's he saying about it? I really hope he approves. We get to be a happy family again."

"Daphne, there's something I need to tell you." My voice croaked as I looked into her now glossy eyes.

RICK

Episode Thirteen

The acrid smoke from the kitchen sent me rushing there. I'd only left the egg to simmer for just a few minutes, only for my house to be almost caught up in smoke. Puffing out cloudy breaths, I turned off the electric stove and stared at the now overly burnt egg. It was so black, the homeless dog that roamed the streets would refuse it.

Cooking isn't for me. I wished I'd taken the art of cooking more seriously when my mother insisted on teaching me. I never had a reason to learn how to cook until now- and I couldn't even succeed in frying an egg.

The doorbell rang, and a frown settled on my face. Who dared knock on my door on this hot summer afternoon? I grabbed my shirt from the counter, a part of me wishing it was Shae standing outside the door. A bigger part of me knew that wouldn't happen in a million years. A week had passed since she last came here. You know, when she helped my drunk ass home, and we had that gut-wrenching conversation which meant I had no chance of ever seeing her again.

Had I learned to accept the Rick and Shae love story had forever ended? No. Yet, there was one thing I accepted. I hurt her, and I should give her the chance to move on. Yes, it'd hurt to see her with someone else, but it'd be better for her to get the love and respect I didn't give her.

I unlocked the door and instantly felt my heart drop into my stomach. In hindsight, I shouldn't have opened the door.

"Hi, Rick."

"Melanie." Wild waves of emotions swirled in me. For a split second, my hands lost their ability to move- and so did my legs. My brain instantly fogged as I began to blink like a battered robot. My heart pounded wildly in my chest as I stared at the figure before me. She smiled and then gestured to come inside. I didn't respond, just moved out of the way to let her pass. When I finally regained the power to speak, I was certain a century had passed.

"Melanie, what are you doing here?" I blinked, then rubbed my tempo, effortlessly displaying how uncomfortable I truly felt. When Shae talked about her sudden appearance in Long Island, I thought she bluffed. Seeing Melanie in her full profile, looking nothing like the girl I knew before, gave me apocalypse vibes.

"Is that how to greet the mother of your child?" She said with a sly smile and slumped groovily onto the couch. For someone I didn't like and wanted absolutely nothing to do with, she sure felt comfortable in my crib. She yanked her sneakers off and dropped her legs onto the counter table, refusing to delete that ugly smile from her face.

"If you came here to see Miranda, she's at a daycare center. I suggest you go, and when she returns, I'll give you a call." I hated that I was lenient with her. Yet, I had no choice. Her leaving town was all because of me.

"No. I came to see you. And of course, our daughter too. We need to talk, Rick." She jumped to her feet, neared me, and pushed me into an unrequited hug. I grimaced as I stood as rigid as a tree. What followed next was that she took my hand and dragged me towards the couch, urging me to sit down.

"So, news around town is, you and Shae broke up. Is that true?" She asked, a twinkle of something I couldn't put my mind to, glistened in her eye. "You don't have to answer. This house doesn't look like it has any feminine presence."

"What do you really want, Melanie?" I asked, suddenly irritated by her voice, her demeanor, and her everything.

"Shae knows that Miranda is our daughter. So, I came with a proposition." She puffed out a breath.

"You're out of your mind if you think you can walk around with any authority card after abandoning her for all these months." I jumped to my feet and lashed out at her through gritted teeth.

"Abandoned her. I didn't abandon her, you asshole? Oh, you think I don't know you were the one that sent me those threats which caused me to leave town. So, don't you dare try to play that victim card on me." She spat out.

"How did you know about that? Have you seen Shae since you got here?"

"You think I've gone to see Shae. No, bruh. And how I got to know is none of your concern. What did you really want, Rick? You'd chase me out of town and live happily ever after with your Shae." She batted her eyes annoyingly. "But I guess Karma hit you harder than I ever would."

"You need to leave," I said, my eyes pleading with hers. I didn't know where Melanie was all this time, but she appeared different. That sweet, calm girl was replaced by the devious Jezebel spirit. It scared and terrified me.

"I said we need to talk. We're not done, and you're asking me to leave?" She asked like I was dumb for making that statement. "The thing is, I'm back in town.

I'm ready to be a mother to Miranda, and it appears you're doing a good job as a daddy."

"Yes, you're Miranda's mother. You get to see her whenever." I said in a defeated tone.

"No. You're not getting my point, Rick. We're a family. You, me, and Miranda."

"What are you saying, Melanie?"

"That I'm glad I didn't abort when you told me to." She got to her feet and leaned towards me, her arms swinging over my neck. "That I'm glad I had Miranda. That I'm glad Shae is out of your life for good since us three, with Miranda, of course, are going to be one sweet, happy family."

"Melanie." My nostrils flared open as I clenched my fist.

"I'm moving in with you and Miranda. What do you think?"

JEROME

Episode Fourteen

"What?" She whispered, looking intently at me. I couldn't stare back at her, so I spun, my back facing her. My inner demons taunted me, and I screeched my fingers over my face. Should I tell her, or I should postpone it for another day? The truth was the latter sounded like the better idea, yet the longer I waited, the harder it'd be for the truth to come out. I gathered every courage that I possessed and spun to face her. "What is it? Why are you being weird?"

"We need to talk," I said, taking her hand, unsure whether to lead her outside or stay indoors. Reasons being I had no idea how this conversation would escalate, but I preferred if the children didn't hear a drop of it.

"Oh my God, your boss rejected your transfer?"

"No. Can we go to the backyard, please?" I gulped down saliva as she gave a single nod. Straddling closely behind her, I didn't miss her occasional head turns. My blood boiled. Sweat incinerated my forehead and every part of my body.

The truth shall set you free, Jerome. Come out and say it.

"So, what did you want to tell me, Jerome?" With folded arms, she titled her head to look at me. I had my face leveled downward, mumblings inarticulate words. She lifted my jaw with a finger, and like magic, the dread spread across my face reflected on hers.

"I did something back in Elmont." I peeked at her, requesting her permission to go on. Her head gave the go-ahead, yet her eyes begged me not to speak.

"What did you do, Jerome?" Her voice croaked. "What did you do?"

"I cheated. I cheated on you." I let out in a low tone. So low I didn't hear myself. "I cheated, and I'm sorry. Daphne, I'm sorry."

"Was that the reason why you kept going there? Why

you couldn't even spend two weeks with your own family?" This wasn't the reaction I expected. Even as she asked these questions, she seemed indifferent, like she expected it all along.

"Yes and no." I breathed out.

"Oh, okay. So, you telling me now means you're no longer with her?"

"Who was she?" She asked, eyes on the ground.

"Just some random girl I met. She's not important. I drew closer to her." A part of me expected her to flinch at my move, but she didn't, and that encouraged me to touch her on the hand. "I wouldn't say that it was a mistake."

"Of course, you can't. You wanted it." She stepped backward, rubbing her forehead. "You know the funny thing in all of this is that I knew. I knew you were cheating, Jerome."

"I'm sorry, Daphne." Tears gathered in my eyes as more shame consumed my body. "I promise to never do anything to hurt you again."

"Did you love her, or she was just pleasing to your

eyes?" Her eyes begged for the truth. I stared down at my hands, hoping to find the right answer. It was a tricky question from Daphne as any answer will mark an underlined factor; I found her attractive.

"We grew close, and one thing led to another."

"You grew close. So, she was there all along. The times you came home to see your family?" She asked, her tone higher now.

"Yes," I said in a monotone. I still had no willpower to look her squarely in the eye. I only subjected my gaze to the grassy ground and the broken rocking chair leaning against the hedge.

"How long did this thing go on for? I'm sorry if I'm asking questions but_."

"I understand, Daphne. It started three months ago. I finally had the courage to say it." A single trickle of tear fell down her eyes. I remained transfixed in my position. I wanted to hold her, but in my chagrin, it would be a stupid move.

"You were sleeping with her for three months? God, this is unbelievable." She chuckled. "You know how ironic life can be sometimes. I'm being faithful and loyal to you- Heck, I'm bragging about how fidelity is your hallmark because I know the people that raised you. Papa and mama John inspired me to stay true to my husband. And you, you just ruined that for me."

"You have to believe me, Daphne. I know what I did, and you have no idea how remorseful I feel."

"That's why you confessed to me, right? Cos, you were so guilty. Your sanity didn't feel right with you?"

"I couldn't live a pretense life of happiness when deep down, I knew I had a giant skeleton in my closet."

"Mom. Dad." Lily's soft voice called out to us. Daphne immediately wiped the tear from her eye and faced Lily, who stood at the door. "Hey honey, what's the problem?"

"Georgie has hidden my dollie. Please tell him to give it to me." She said.

"Okay, honey. Mommy will be there soon." She gave Lily a smile, then turned to me. "I think we're going to need some space from each other."

And with that, she disappeared from sight.

RICK

Episode Fifteen

"I think you're out of your mind." I let out, my breaths, a miscalculated intake of air. "You aren't moving in with anyone."

"I wasn't asking you, Rick. Now, don't make me sound like a crazy bitch." She sighed, shaking her head slightly.

"You *are* a crazy woman. You just can't walk into my home and decide to move in." I paced my room, wondering what I did to deserve this. Who would have thought one slip-up could cause this turmoil in my life. So many thoughts ran through my head, I literally felt my head become hot. I ran my palms over my face, muttering inarticulate words as they were at that moment, my coping mechanism.

"I can. I'm the mother of your child. I have every right

to. You can't kick me out; I'll report you to the police."

I chuckled, hovering my hands over my lips. "You're going to blackmail me now?"

"Just grow up, Rick, and stop being a fucking baby. What's it going to cost you if I live here?"

"I don't love you," I whispered silently.

"Oh, please." She rolled her eyes before sauntering to the kitchen to fetch a bottle of water from the fridge. "Spare me that crap. Love? I don't need your love, Rick. You think you men are capable of love? What you think is love, isn't, honey. You all claim to love a woman until another woman strips naked in front of you. You suddenly lose the meaning of that love, so don't you dare stand there and preach to me about love."

"Yes, Melanie. I know. I know I fucked up, and it's really been eye-opening. But, lemme tell you one thing, I do love Shae."

"I don't care if you love Shae." The bitterness in her voice was so disdain. "I'm here for my daughter, whom you drove me to abandon. We're are going to be good examples to our daughter, so don't be all bitter towards me. We don't want our child having abandonment issues when she grows up." She pointed out to me. "Where do I sleep?"

Ignoring her, I darted to my bedroom, changed into another shirt, and evacuated the door. I heard her nasty laughter even as I ignited the engine of my car. If it wasn't for the years of pain I'd endured, I'd have burst into tears. Refusing to stoop low for this sudden phase in my life, I drove to Shae's house. I had no explanation for heading toward her house, but she was my safe haven. It wasn't something I could explain. It just was.

My car came to its usual halt, and in a nanosecond, I rammed my body out of the car. Irritation, frustration, bitterness, and anger all crawled up my skin, taking every little space of sanity I had left. Shae. Shae was the only one who could restore my sanity back into place. I pounded on her door like a deranged person until the door opened.

"What is it? Why are you pounding on my door, and what the hell are you even doing here?" She asked, not the least pleased to see me. She folded her arms on her chest and looked intently at me. I knew she saw my distress but the old Shae that cared for me and would hug me was gone. This new Shae just stood there, indifferent and irritated at my presence. "What do you want, Rick? I'm going out soon, so."

"Going out? With who?" The question flew sharply out of my mouth. "You know what, forget I asked."

"Good, cos it doesn't concern you. What are you doing here?" She asked, her arms folded on her chest.

"Melanie is here," I said, pacing the porch and missing her reaction. I spun, and her eyes bulged in surprise.

"Here... here as in?"

"She's in my apartment, Shae." I let out in a shrill voice.

"Oh, okay. So, what are you doing here, or you came to inform me? If you're wondering if I've seen her, I haven't. I knew she was back in Long Island, but I was clueless on where she really was at."

"She's talking crazy. Talking about moving in with me. About wanting to be a family. I can't go back there."

"Why did you come to me with this? You do know

that she's the reason for our breakup, and you thought it was a good idea for you to drive all that way to come tell me this? Why?"

"I don't know. I don't know. I guess you're the only person I can share my burden with. She knows everything. She knows we're not together anymore. She knows I was the one who sent her those messages."

"I see. So, what are you going to do about it?"

"I don't know, Shae. I don't think I can get rid of her." I said, and Shae gave a knowing smile.

"Of course, you can't. She's Miranda's mother. No matter what, Melanie is a part of your life now."

"I know. To be honest, I have no problem with that. She wants to be in Miranda's life, fine, but I can't imagine my life with her." I said, and Shae threw her head at me. We locked stares for a brief moment before she cleared her throat and looked away. "She won't leave cos she has leverage on me."

"The messages?"

"Yes. She said she'll tell the cops if I don't let her move in with me."

"Listen, Rick, I'm sorry you're going through all this, but there's nothing I can do."

"Can I stay here for a few nights?" The question flew out of my mouth.

"What?" She asked, taken aback.

"Can I stay with you for a couple of nights? Just for me to clear my head and think of the next move. If I go back to my house with her in there, I'll go insane."

"What about Miranda?"

"I'll know what to do with her?"

"Rick, I... I can't. We've broken up." She shuddered, and it made me wonder if missing me was a factor in that.

"I know. I promise to keep my distance."

"Distance where? My room has only one bed and no couch."

"I'll sleep on the floor. Please, Shae."

She sighed a breath and nodded. "Fine. For only one night, though."

JEROME

Episode Sixteen

I'd spent the past couple of days isolated in a hotel room. I hadn't stepped out in those number of days. My entire world had come crashing down, and I allowed it. I understood I was human and prone to mistakes. I also knew I wasn't the first man to cheat. That, however, didn't make me feel better. It only added me to the statistical analysis that men were actual scumbags, undeserving of genuine love. In the past forty-eight hours, I hadn't called Daphne. Neither had she. Which meant in the past forty-eight hours, I hadn't spoken to my kids or seen them.

Daphne said she needed space, and I was clueless about what the outcome would be. For starters, I attested to the fact that my marriage was over. There was no way Daphne would be with a cheating husband. I knew she loved me. She loved the family we'd created, yet she deserved to be treated better. And heavens knew if she gave me another chance, I'd treasure and cherish her even more. I'd treat her and our marriage with the utmost love and respect.

Daphne wasn't the first woman I dated, but she was the only woman I genuinely loved. After nine months of dating, I was ready to tie the knots with her. My commitment to her was something I didn't quite believe I possessed. Before her, I was quite the ladies' man. I didn't do relationships, something my parents saw as a disease, and spent months, possibly years, looking for a cure. When I finally introduced Daphne to them, they were taken aback yet completely overjoyed.

Our wedding day was truly the happiest moment of my life. I recalled every single moment like it was just yesterday. It was, however, extremely funny how these moments resurfaced in my head now that I was on the verge of losing her. Daphne looked so beautiful in her white gown. Even better to our story, she was pregnant with Georgie.

Nothing made me happier.

And for a split second, I wished I could relive that moment again.

My phone rang, subjecting me to a full-blown panic attack. I rushed for it underneath the pillow with a part of me hoping- praying it was Daphne. Instead, it was my parents. Grief washed over me as it instantly hit me why they called. Heaving a sigh, I slammed the phone to my ears.

"Son." My father's strong voice came at me. "I want you to come home now. Wherever you are."

"Dad. I_"

"Don't say a word, and drive your ass home, right now." He emphasized each word, and I knew best not to argue with him. Begrudgingly, I got up from the floor after we hung up, dusted myself, and shoved my body out of the door. I wore the same clothes that I walked into this hotel with- and that was two days ago.

I slid into the elevator, and within seconds, I evacuated the building. The drive to my parents' house undoubtedly filled me with anxiety. It was clear they'd figured it out. I didn't blame Daphne for informing them. My parents would have sucked the truth out of her regardless. I knew they'd be disappointed. I braced myself for whatever they had for me.

When I arrived at their house, my father was on the porch, bent over the parapet. I swallowed a huge gulp of air at his sight, and he stood upright and scrunched his face in a tight expression.

"Good afternoon, dad." I greeted, looking everywhere but him. "I know you know that_" My sentence was left midway when my mother opened the door, the same tight expression on her face. I inhaled sharply, knowing this wasn't going to get any better. "I'm not proud of what I did."

"She wants a divorce." My mother said, breaking eye contact with me faster than the speed of light. My face dropped, along with my heart. I expected this, but finally hearing the confirmation broke my heart all over.

"We didn't call you here to judge you, son. You have

a family. A beautiful family. I don't think you want to lose that, do you?" My father looked intently at me. My mother leaned closer to him as he placed his hands over her shoulders.

"No, father. I wouldn't want to."

"The truth is, son, we all make mistakes. We're not condoning what you did, which I should say was really bad and selfish of you, but you can always right the wrong. Daphne wants a divorce, but I believe you can change her mind about it. You can ask for her forgiveness, which won't be easy but worth it." My mother offered.

"I'll do everything in my power. I wouldn't want to lose her or my children."

"That's all we wanted to hear." My father said with a soft smile on his face. My mother neared me and pushed me into a warm embrace.

"I'm sorry for disappointing you. And I promise_" They held up their hands simultaneously to stop me from speaking.

"The only person who needs to see that change is

Daphne and not us."

I gave an affirmative nod. My phone rang again from my back pocket. In a rush, I picked it up, still hoping it was Daphne. It was my boss. I excused myself from my parents while I picked the call.

"Jerome, good afternoon. Sorry you haven't heard from me. Hope you're good?"

"Yes, sir. I'm doing well." There was no point in explaining my actual well-being to my boss. Odds were, he didn't care, and I didn't feel like sharing. "I take it that you have news for me."

"Yes. Your transfer has been approved. You can start work in New Jersey now." He said. Even though I was supposed to be happy, I didn't feel that emotion.

"Thank you, sir, for giving me this chance."

"You start work on Monday." He said, and we hung up.

I turned to my parents, who still had their eyes on me. "My transfer just got approved. Looks like that's fate's way of saying everything will be fine."

RICK

Episode Seventeen

"So, you're saying she has allowed you to spend the night at her place?" Dennis asked as he dropped the controller on the cushion. I was currently at his place since I couldn't stay with Shae, and I had no desire to go back to my house with Melanie there. I had already made arrangements for Miranda. Just like how I was to spend the night with Shae, Miranda would be with the nanny. "I see." He said with a sly smile.

"What?" I asked, trying to decode the mischievous look on his face.

"Oh, nothing, I'm just wondering why you didn't come to me. You know I'd let you crash here for as long as you want, yet you went back to the one person you claimed to be avoiding. Mmm." He rubbed his jaw like solving a difficult science question.

He had a point. In fact, thinking about it now, I should have asked Dennis instead. "Yeah, you're right. But I was so mad, and my emotions were all over the place."

"You were so mad that the only person that came to mind was Shae. It's cool. I understand." He laughed, reaching for the controller and resuming the game. "I have one question, though, is it for this night only?"

"Yes, it is. Mentally, I'm not prepared to meet Melanie, so I might come crash here."

"Yeah, your second option is always opened to you." He smirked.

"Shut up, man." I checked the time, and it was seven. The cover of nightfall had blanketed the sky, which meant I had to head home. I had to admit, I was nervous going back to Shae's place. Different scenarios played in my head on how I'd love the night to pan out. "Okay, man, I have to leave now."

Dennis gave me a goofy smile, then burst into laughter. "Alright, sure. Go home. I'm sure it's past your curfew."

"Shut up, man. I'll see you tomorrow." Giving him a manly handshake, I turned towards the door. "What do you think I should do about Melanie?"

"She sounds real crazy now. I don't want to get in her way. But I'm sure we'll find a way to get rid of her." I narrowed my eyes at him. "Not that way, but if we have to stoop to that, I'll help you get rid of her body."

"Real funny, man. Bye." And with that, I scurried out of the house. On my way to Shae's apartment, I wanted to call and ask what food she preferred since I was getting some take-home for myself. I shrugged against the idea and bought two take-outs. One thing that I knew about Shae was that she loved her food. That was her love language. I recalled times I'd piss her off, and only food, specifically sea-boiled food, could calm her down. I got two Chinese and drove home.

The door was locked when I turned the knob, but it didn't take a minute before she opened it. She was donned in comfy pajamas, her braids atop her head in a messy style. Her lips stood out as she'd applied lip gloss.

At that moment, I wished it was just like old times. I would grab her and kiss her, and she'd giggle in my ears.

"I got Chinese," I said after an infinity of ogling her.

"Oh, okay." She peered at me and moved out the door. I entered the little space, and my eyes followed her as she slumped on the bed. "I'm not hungry, so you can put that in the fridge."

"Sure." I paced the room like it was my first time being here. It did feel like my first time being here. I kicked my sneakers away and plopped my ass on the carpeted floor. My back faced her, and I wondered if she peeked momentarily at me.

Silence filled the room as I ate, and she pressed her phone. Every two minutes that passed, a soft cackle erupted from her, and I wondered who made her laugh. I'd know if it was a funny video. It wasn't.

"Can you please turn off the lights when you're done eating?" She said after thirty minutes of deafening silence. I gave her an affirmative nod as I had just finished with my food. I got up and cleared the space, which was to be my bed space.

"Here," she threw a comforter and a pillow at me. "It can get cold sometimes." She said before turning to face the wall.

"Thanks," I said as I flicked the light off, and darkness reigned in the room. My phone vibrated, and I reached for it from my front pocket. It was a text from Dennis. I only shook my head and shut it off. I didn't know how long it was until I felt a tap on my stomach.

"Okay, I'm feeling bad for making you sleep on the floor. So, you can join me on the bed."

I gulped. Did she just_ "No, Shae. I'm fine. I promised to respect your privacy."

"So, you're okay on the floor?"

"Well, it's not the comfiest place, but it's only for this night."

"Okay. At least I offered." She whispered.

You fool.

Seconds turned into minutes, and an inner war was waged within me. I heaved a sigh of defeat as I hopped from the floor and onto the bed. In my quest to be as quiet as possible, I failed when the bed creaked as I crawled into it.

The windows reflected a soft brilliance of the evening light. From where I slept, I made out every feature of Shae. The dark glow that peeked from the window ricocheted on her skin, granting a very beautiful skin shade. I longed to touch, but that would gift me a slap.

"What made you change your mind?" She tossed to face me, and I couldn't even pretend not to be staring at her.

JEROME

Episode Eighteen

For the first time in my life, I entered my own house with a heavy heart. The days of me treading in and out easily were over. I felt like a stranger in my own abode. I spent seven days at the hotel. My parents advised me to wait for Daphne's call before I made any attempt to show my undesired face at home. I had to wait seven days for that. She wanted me to come over so that we could have a conversation.

I hadn't informed her of my job permanency in New Jersey. Maybe after what she had to say, I could tell her. It'd been five minutes since I arrived. Lily and Georgie were at my parents' place, sparing the needed time for Daphne and me to have a mature conversation.

She handed me a glass of orange juice before

slumping on the couch. It was hard to discern her actual feelings as Daphne had always been the type to conceal her emotions. She wore a slight touch of make-up on her face, enhancing her beauty and, for some odd reasons, raising my insecurity to another level.

"Thank you for agreeing to come." She said, clearing her throat before setting her own glass of juice on the table. It felt incredibly weird that my wife and I had come to this. She sat across me like she was a therapist and me, her client. I didn't say much as I knew I was the cause of all of this. If only I had been loyal. "Papa and Mama told me that your request to work here has been approved." Of course, trust my parents to always leak information.

I nodded. "Yes. I started on Monday. What have you told the kids about me?"

"That you had to travel. You wanted to say goodbye, but it was too urgent, and you had to leave." She stared at her hands while she spoke, only lifting her head to me at the end of every sentence.

"Oh, okay. I thought you'd told them."

"No, I wouldn't do that." She gave me a weak smile. "You're their father. What happens between us should not affect them. And I'll never ruin you to them."

"But if you decide to divorce me, we'd have to tell them the truth." I had no idea why the words flowed so effortlessly from my mouth while my heart bled with every syllabus.

"You think I'll divorce you?" She asked with a raised eyebrow.

"You won't?" I narrowed my eyes at her. "If I'm being honest with you, Daphne, before coming here, I'd already predicted how this meeting would be."

"And part of your prediction is that I'll divorce you?"

I rubbed my hands over my face, unsure what to say to not come off as a complete dork. "I know you. I know what you'll tolerate and won't tolerate."

She nodded. "Yes, you're right. But I also have something to confess."

I squinted my eyes at her, surprised at what she had just said. She exhaled sharply, then clasped both hands together. She shut her eyes for approximately five seconds before fluttering them open and turning to me with bleak eyes.

"A month into our relationship, I_."

"You also cheated?" I blurted out without thinking.

She shook her head vehemently. "No, I've never cheated on you before, Jerome. The thing is, a month in our relationship, I got pregnant." She looked at me like she was waiting for a response. When none came, she continued, "I got pregnant."

"It was mine?"

"Yes." She whispered. "I wasn't ready to have a baby yet. I wasn't ready. Our relationship was new. I had no idea how things would end for us, so..... I had an abortion."

"What?" I gasped.

"I wanted to tell you. I really did, but when we got married, and we had Lily and George, I figured what the hell. We've been able to have children. The past didn't matter anymore."

I couldn't believe the words she had just uttered. I shut my eyes, hoping that would help me process the information that had been dropped on me.

"When you told me you cheated, I knew I couldn't hold it against you knowing I had my own skeleton in the closet."

"If I hadn't cheated, would you have ever told me?"

After a long silence came the reply I dreaded. "No. I wouldn't have." She wiped the tears from her eyes. "I'm sorry. I should have told you right from the start."

"But why didn't you?"

"I was scared. I didn't know how you were going to react. It was only a month, Jerome."

I got up from my couch and advanced toward her. Holding her up, I wiped the tears from her eyes. The truth was we both had no right to judge the other. I wanted to be angry at her after what she confessed, yet I couldn't, knowing I'd equally wronged her.

"I'm sorry, Jerome. The truth is, when you told me you cheated, I couldn't even get angry at you."

"No, Daphne. You had every right to be angry at me. Even though we've faulted each other, they are very different transgressions."

"So, you forgive me?"

"I do. I'm hoping we can move past all of this and start afresh with our beautiful children."

"Yes."

"And that henceforth, there'd be no secrets. We'll tell each other everything."

"Yes." She broke into a fit of sobs, and I pulled her into my arms. In my honest opinion, everything was easier said than done. If we were going to bury the past, six feet underneath us, a lot of work and effort were needed.

Both of our wounds were opened, and time was needed to make them heal completely.

RICK

Episode Ninteen

"The bed's warmer," I whispered, and I heard her chuckle in the darkness. She shifted, and I did the same, inching our bodies closer. "Thank you for letting me sleep here tonight."

"It's fine. No problem." She sighed. Silence engulfed us once again. Unlike before, this was a comfortable silence. I reached for my phone from the floor and played soft musical melodies. I heard her hum along with one melody, and I couldn't help but smile. "You don't want us to sleep?"

"I think the purpose of these songs is to help you sleep," I whispered. "Besides, you're the one humming along with it."

She chuckled. "I know. I can't help it." She laid on her

back, her eyes facing the ceiling. "Where did you take Miranda?"

"She's with Amelia, the nanny."

"You can't keep her from Melanie forever, you know. You're only going to make your case worse."

"I'm not going to do that. I simply want her out of my house." I let out an exasperated breath, and Shae chortled. "You know, she said something. I can't seem to forget it."

"What did she say?" Shae asked, tossing away from the ceiling and facing me.

I huffed. "I told her she couldn't stay at my house cos I didn't love her. I don't know why but I figured me saying something like that would scurry her out of my house. She told me she didn't care about that. And that a man's love is always up to a point."

"Was she right, though?"

"No. She isn't. I understand that men are moved by what we see. We do fall short when we see other attractive women, but a man's love is never up to a certain point. Most men love unconditionally."

"Ohkay." She let out. Either she wasn't interested in what I said, or she didn't understand the point I tried to make. "You said that she knew about everything when she came over?"

"Yes."

"I guess that's the reason she couldn't come here." Shae scoffed. "Well, I guess Melanie and I have come to our final destination."

"I'm really sorry, Shae. I know you loved her." I reached and touched her arm. When she didn't flinch, I allowed it to linger there.

"I loved you more, Rick." She whispered, sparing me a quick glance before ultimately breaking eye contact.

"I love_."

"Please, don't say anything. Let's just sleep, okay."

"Shae, no. I know I messed up. But I never lied when I said I loved you. I love you. And what happened that night with Melanie is the worst thing to happen to me. It shouldn't have happened. I shouldn't have gotten that drunk. I'm sorry, Shae. I don't think I'll ever love anyone as much as I love you. I can't imagine my life without you in it." The pain in my heart was so unbearable I thought I would die. It was etched in my heart like a stone. The right thing for me to do was to let her go as I promised before, but the truth was, I couldn't. I had no idea how my life would be without Shae in it. I didn't want to think about it. I wanted her in my present and future.

"Rick."

"I'm so sorry, baby. I'm sorry." I whispered against her cheek. We were so close now. Only a thin gap of air separated us. "I want you. I want us forever."

"I love you, Rick. For the past few weeks, I tried hating you, but I just can't. I wanted to hate you so much." I moved a finger to wipe the tear from her eyes. "I love you so much to hate you."

"I don't want you to ever hate me."

"God, I miss you so much." She breathed against my lips. Her breath instantly intoxicated me. With her continuous heavy breathing, her lips touched mine. Seconds passed, and our lips glazed with each other's. I wanted to kiss her. Heavens knew the minute her lips touched mine, I lost my mind. Yet, I didn't want to cause panic in her. I didn't want to terrify her or push her away. She sucked on my lower lips, and I responded almost immediately. The fire in our kiss could cause an explosion. She forced her tongue into my mouth, and I granted her full access. Pushing her body against mine, it became clear she missed me just as much as I missed her. Our kiss continued in its fiery passion as my hand caressed her entire body.

"God, I miss you so much." She muttered against my lips before taking them again.

"I miss you too, Shae." I rolled on top of her, our tongues still entwined. She snaked her arms around my neck, burying me deeper into her. My lips left hers and connected with her neck, her collarbone, her ears, then back to her lips. My hand discovered her breast as I kneaded it softly. She let out a moan that made my groin kick wildly in my jeans. She opened the buttons on my shirt and removed it from my body. I did same with her pajamas until she lay naked underneath me.

"You sure about this?" It was important I double-checked. In as much as I loved the skin-to-skin sensation, I didn't want her to regret this.

Her eyes turned glossy as she looked at me. She pulled my head closer and pressed her lips to mine. "You're asking like it's my first time."

"I don't want you to regret it, Shae." I stared deeply into her eyes. "Damn it, I love you."

"I love you too, Rick. I don't think I'm ready to let go of everything yet." The words were like music to my ears. To hear Shae profess her love for me was as if a million years had been added to my life.

"I'm ready to fight for us."

"What about Melanie? It looks like she's not going away anytime soon." She muttered.

"Don't worry about her. All I want is you, Shae. Only you." For the first time in weeks, she smiled. I kissed her gently, shifting myself perfectly between her widely opened legs. "Melanie won't come between us ever again."

She nodded, holding my head steadily in her hand. I rammed into her, remembering how delicious she'd always been and how lucky I was to finally have her back.

And even though Melanie was still a much bigger itch to be scratched, all that mattered now was Shae.

JEROME

Episode Twenty

One month later.

* * *

"What's wrong, honey?" After minutes of searching for Lily, I found her hiding behind the refrigerator, muffling quiet sounds of tears and clutching her dollie tightly on her chest. I urged her to come out of her little hiding place. I had to be honest; I was completely taken aback by her reaction. Today was her sixth birthday, and when Daphne and I organized this grand birthday celebration for her, we didn't expect her to be seeking refuge behind the refrigerator. She sniffed, wiping her face with the dollie and nearing me. She kept her gaze down, so I bent to her level. “What's wrong, Lily? Everybody is waiting for you to cut the cake. Why have you come to hide here?”

"I want to go to Red Lobster. I don't want a party." She sobbed, finally lifting her head to look at me.

I chuckled silently, careful not to let her see. "You want to go to Red Lobster. I'll take you to Red Lobster after the party."

Her eyes lit up. “Really?"

"Yes. Now, why don’t you go and cut your cake. Everyone is waiting for you.” She nodded happily and skidded away. I gave my head a playful shake, elated to see the birthday girl high in her spirits.

I sauntered back to the backyard where the party was thrown. Words couldn't describe the peace that dwelled in me. I'd become more light-weighted, more fulfilled, and genuinely content. A whole month had passed since Daphne and I chose to put the past behind us and start anew. I had to admit, it wasn't easy in the beginning. We both made complete fools of ourselves, trying so hard to forget our transgressions. What we failed to understand was, regardless of our quest to be a happy family once again, it wasn't easy to forget.

After a week of feigning perfections, we decided to resort to therapy. Our sessions were still ongoing, and to our delight, there'd been massive improvements. We no longer put on charades. We communicated better, and we were on the road to being a strong, formidable pair.

"What was wrong with her?" Daphne came to stand beside me at the feet of the door.

"She wants to go to Red Lobster," I answered, and she gasped, causing me to laugh. We headed back inside the kitchen. “I told her after the party, we'd go.”

"I can't believe she cried because of that." Daphne expressed.

"I understand her. It's obviously what she wanted." I shrugged as I plonked on the barstool.

"It could have also saved us a lot of money if we'd spoken to her about what she wanted for her birthday."

"Yeah, that would have been the best." Daphne laughed. "We're bad parents for that. We were wrong to assume. Georgie loved his birthday party last year, so we thought_."

"Lily would love one too." She cut in.

"Lily is about to cut her cake. What are you two doing here." My mom stuck her head through the kitchen door and scorned us.

"Sure, we'll be there in a minute," I responded, jumping to my feet and grabbing Daphne's hand.

"There's something I need to tell you." She said as her throat bobbed. "But I can do that after the birthday."

"Is it serious?" I quirked my eyebrow.

She smiled and shook her head. "No. It can wait."

I kissed her on the tempo, and we scurried out of the kitchen to the backyard. We didn't invite a lot of people as Lily didn't have enough friends. Most of the invited guests were our neighbors. The birthday song was chanted, shifting the ambiance of the atmosphere to be more cheerful and jaunty.

"Happy birthday to the prettiest princess in the world." My father screamed, bouncing Lily in the air. Together with my mother, they went up to the cake, and with a big smile on Lily's face, she cut it. Thunderous claps reigned the entire space.

"Dad, can we go to Red lobster now," Lily said with icing all over her lips.

"Yes, honey, we will." I hugged her and released her almost immediately. I searched around for Daphne. A part of me wondered what she had to tell me. Even though she said it was nothing to be worried about, my heart raced faster just thinking about it.

"Honey," I called out to her as she spoke to one of our neighbors.

"Hey. I was looking for you." She grabbed my hand and dragged me from the horde. Using another door, we came to the front of the house and slid into the living room.

She urged me to sit down as she fell right beside me on the couch.

"What is it? You're making me nervous." I gave a soft laugh, looking at her.

"Okay, I think it's best I show it to you." Giggling, she jerked onto her feet and disappeared upstairs. Minutes later, her footfalls thundered on the stairs as she descended. There was a brown envelope in her hand. My brain traveled to all scenarios to which a brown envelope would mean. She slumped in the seat beside me and handed the envelope. Squaring my eyes at her, I tore the envelope open and patiently read its content.

"Really?" I gasped.

"Yes. I'm pregnant." She burst into a peal of laughter amid the silent tears that flowed.

"That's amazing." My heart leaped in my chest at the thought of a new member of the family.

"You're happy about this?"

"Yes, why wouldn't I be? This is amazing. Thank you." I held her and kissed her tenderly. You couldn't have made me happier.

She held me tightly. "I didn't know what to expect. I know we're going through a rough time, and I wasn't sure how you'd respond to_."

"I love you," I said and kissed her. "We need to celebrate."

"I could use some Red Lobster too." She said with a laugh.

"Let's go get some for you and our babies."

SHAE~THE END

Episode Twenty One

EPILOGUE

A year later

* * *

All's well that ends well.

If anyone had told me what the outcome of my life was, a year before what I felt to be the greatest conundrum to ever happen to me, I wouldn't have believed.

Not the slightest bit.

Yet, in retrospect, I was glad for everything that happened. I did wonder why such bad things could happen to me regardless of my kindness to others. I lost my best friend, Melanie. And the great love story Rick and I once built.

It was a road I wanted to avoid forever. A chapter of my life I wanted shut and burnt in the fire. I could never relive those moments I went through. The emotional trauma and physical attacks I faced were ones that now ascribed me as *strong*. The struggle and fight for love were hard. Regardless of how much Rick loved me or how I loved him, it was extremely difficult getting the snake out of his home- out of his life.

It was then I discovered a brand new side to Melanie. Her resilience was both impressive, and detestable. For someone I'd known for so long, her blatant display of hatred towards me was one I never thought I'd see. I mean, I knew I had enemies but, Melanie? No way. She proved me wrong when she made attempts to get Rick and me out of the way.

Rick had his fair share of reproach when Melanie exposed him for sending her away. Coming from a wealthy home, Rick was able to clean his name fair and square.

Melanie fell flat on her face when the war ended. She

stuck around for a while and directed her anger at me.

For a whole month, I became hospitalized from an ambush she set up for me. Clearly, a wonder how I was alive today.

My life had been a roller coaster of a ride, and this all happened in a year.

Back then, I regretted everything and everyone. I regretted the day I met Melanie, took her in, and called her my friend. I regretted Rick. Through all that battle, he proved his love for me. It was in this moment of hopelessness that he held my hand and promised to be there.

A year and our love had grown stronger than ever before. We got married two months ago and nothing made me happier.

I had to admit, on the level of trust, my grade was an average. I believed as time-lapsed and with more reasons, I'd learn to trust him fully.

There were times I shuddered at the reflection of the past- memories resurfacing of Rick and Melanie. It was nightmarishly scary and devouring. The only part of me that relaxed was the knowledge of Melanie's disappearance. Nobody knew where she was, and quite frankly, I- we preferred it as such.

I looked down at my flat belly and the brown envelope in my hands and tears welled in them. A car horn interrupted my sentimental moment and I threw my head up to glance at the person. My heart thumped when I saw Rick's mother. Truth was I didn't expect her here, especially at this time. I raised to my feet and neared the wooden stairs that led to our house. In her arms was Miranda, soundly asleep. A smile came to my lips as she laid Miranda on the hammock, advanced toward me, and hugged me.

Yes, I know exactly what you're thinking. Rick's mother finally accepted me. How did this happen? All thanks and praises went to Melanie. In her quest to tear me down and rupture my soul, Rick’s mother- Diana became my second pillar.

"How are you doing, darling?" She asked, cupping my cheeks in her hand. Diana was an amazing mother. I hated how we got off on the wrong foot. She served as a mother figure and more. At this point, she was also my friend. We spent most of our time together, while *our men* went to work. "Were you able to go to the hospital?"

"Yes, I did," I said, tucking both lips in my mouth. “You won't believe it.” I galloped to the armchair I sat in before, grabbed the brown envelope, and flashed it in her face.

"Don't tell me what it is." She asked and I nodded briskly with tears eyeing from my eyes.

"Miranda is about to have a baby brother or sister." She hugged me and we cried together.

The next couple of hours waiting for Rick's return were agonizing. One reason being, Diana basically started treating me like a toddler. Exactly how she treated Miranda. She made me stay idly in the living room while she cooked.

Then suddenly the door clicked to reveal Rick. I jumped on my feet and rushed into his arm. He greeted me with the welcome kiss- as he always did.

"I missed you too, baby. Where's Miranda?" He asked, as she took his bag and placed it on the counter.

"Playing with her toys at the dining table," I said.

Oh, you're here." Diana stuck her head from the kitchen

"Mom, what are you doing here?" Rick asked then gave nervous laughter as Diana's facial expression was epic. "I mean, you're still here?"

"Yes, I'm making dinner. We have good news to celebrate." She nudged me on the shoulder and I gave her a smug look. Way to sell me out, mother-in-law. "Shae has something to tell you."

"What is it, love?" Rick's warm hands enveloped mine and I instantly melted into butter.

“Okay, wait here.” I turned to run upstairs but Diana's voice stopped me.

"Wait. I have it here." She said.

"Oh c’mon, mom." I frowned, settling my arms over my sore breasts. In hindsight, I shouldn't have told her. *Such a buzz kill.*

"No way." Rick gasped when Diana pushed the envelope into his hand. I'm no expert but I know what this means. "Are we pregnant?"

I loved the choice of pronoun he used. It made tears fill in my eyes as he neared me and pushed me into his arms. “This is a sign I'm a good father.”

"You are and a good husband too." I kissed his cheek.

"Miranda is about to be a big sis." Rick cheered.

"Exactly what she said." Diana chipped in. “Like I said, this calls for a celebration.”

"We couldn't agree less." Rick and I said in unison.

The End

www.ingramcontent.com/pod-product-compliance
Lightning Source LLC
LaVergne TN
LVHW041104150826
845673LV00007B/1916